*Zu meine Mudder und Vadder,*
*die auch Deitch sind*
            *—R. A.*


*To my family*
            *—P. P.*


*The author would like to thank Abner, Sara,*
*Lydia, Fannie, and his editor, Marcia Marshall.*

Atheneum Books for Young Readers
An imprint of Simon & Schuster Children's Publishing Division
1230 Avenue of the Americas
New York, New York 10020
Text copyright © 1996 by Richard Ammon
Illustrations copyright © 1996 by Pamela Patrick
All rights reserved including the right of reproduction in whole or in part in any form.
Book design by Becky Terhune
The text of this book is set in Weiss.
The illustrations are rendered in pastels.
First Edition
Printed in the United States of America
10   9   8   7   6   5   4   3   2   1
Library of Congress Cataloging-in-Publication Data
Ammon, Richard.
An Amish Christmas / by Richard Ammon ; illustrated by Pamela Patrick.—1st ed.
        p.    cm.
Summary: Some Amish children celebrate Christmas in their one-room
school and in their own simple ways with their family and relatives.
ISBN 0-689-80377-X
[1. Amish—Fiction.  2. Christmas—Fiction.]  I. Patrick, Pamela, ill.  II. Title.
PZ7.A5165An     1996
[Fic]—dc20
95-33383

# AN AMISH CHRISTMAS

BY RICHARD AMMON

ILLUSTRATED BY PAMELA PATRICK

ATHENEUM BOOKS FOR YOUNG READERS

$M$y little sister, Rachel, and I walk down the lane between the fields, just like most mornings. But today is special. It's Christmas Eve and today we have our Christmas program at school.

When we see Sugar Maple School at the end of the lane, Rachel runs ahead to join a group of girls who play hide-and-seek. As I reach the schoolyard, my friend, Ike, tosses me a ball and the other boys scatter. I guess I'm "It."

Soon Anna, our teacher, rings the bell and we all tramp inside. I hang my black hat and coat on hooks to the right of the door. Rachel and the girls hang their black coats, shawls, and blue bonnets on hooks to the left. We put our lunchboxes on shelves above our coats.

Anna has built a roaring fire in the stove, so the room feels toasty warm. Then she takes attendance. One by one all thirty-two of us in eight grades answer, "Present."

After Anna reads from the Bible, we file to the front of the room to sing "Joy to the World" instead of our usual favorite, "This Land Is Your Land."

Back in our seats, we scholars have trouble keeping our minds on schoolwork.

On most days we play outside after lunch, but today we stay in to get ready. Ike and I string a cord from the east windows to a hook above the chalkboards. Over it we drape a sheet for a curtain.

Rachel and Katie hang letters spelling "Merry Christmas" across the front of the room. Danny and John set out folding chairs and benches for visitors who will soon be coming.

All week Lydia and Malinda have been drawing Christmas scenes with colored chalk on the blackboard. In the center the girls write "Merry Christmas to All" around a picture of candle.

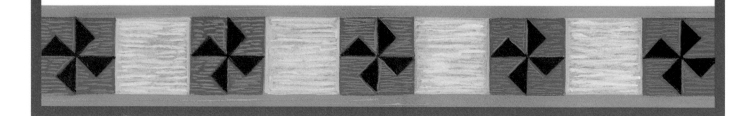

Shortly after noon, some gray buggies drive into the schoolyard. In come the visitors—Mamm, Grossdawdy and Grossmommy, my older sister, Fannie, other mothers and fathers, babies, and a few English friends who were specially invited.

Anna taps the little bell on her desk, and we quickly take our seats. The room becomes quiet. Without prompting, Rachel goes to the front of the room and begins to recite a poem, "Baby Jesus Went to Sleep."

After saying the last line she looks at Anna, who smiles. Relieved, Rachel returns to her seat to enjoy the rest of the program.

We grow up speaking Pennsylvania Dutch, a dialect of German, but in school we speak only English. Just this one time, Anna lets us perform a funny play in Pennsylvania Dutch about a wife who loses the train tickets for a family trip. We laugh when she takes out her handkerchief and the tickets flutter to the floor.

After the first graders recite poems and older scholars perform another skit, the program closes with singing. Ike's mother sings the first notes of "Silent Night" and everyone joins in. When we finish, someone else begins another carol.

After the singing, we give each other gifts. I give a pen that writes in six colors to Sadie. Then Ike places a present on my desk. It's a new Western paperback.

*"Danke* (thank you)," I say.

Anna has an orange and a candy cane filled with candy for each of us. I say, "Thank you, Anna," and hand her my gift, some pink writing paper and envelopes.

Today, Rachel and I do not have to walk home. We climb into our gray buggy, and as Mamm gives the lines a snap, I call to Ike, *"Glick salich Grishtaag* (A most blessed Christmas)."

Ike answers, *"S'nehmlich zu dich* (The same to you)."

I hope I will see Ike on Christmas day or the day after, the Second Day of Christmas.

On a farm Christmas Eve is like any other day. Mamm serves supper about four o'clock before chores. It's dark when Rachel runs off to feed the chickens. I help Fannie and our brother Jake with the milking. As I feed the cows, I hum "The Friendly Beasts."

After cleaning up, I sample some Christmas cookies. During the past week the women met every afternoon in each other's kitchens to bake batches of cookies—sugar cookies cut in different shapes, sand tarts, and chocolate chip cookies. Fannie helped, and when the women came to our house, Rachel got to lick the spoons.

Before going to bed, I look out my bedroom window. *"Siss am schneea* (It's snowing)," I cry. Rachel rushes to the window to look, too. What a perfect Christmas!

At five o'clock on Christmas morning, I hop out of bed, get dressed and go downstairs. But it is not to see what is under the Christmas tree. We don't have a Christmas tree or any other decorations in our homes. Christmas morning is like any other morning for an Amish farmer. The cows must be milked. The animals must be fed.

But I'm first out the door because I want to shovel the path to the barn.

As I wash up after milking, I can smell bacon sizzling. Breakfast isn't ready yet. Instead, presents are piled on the kitchen table. In the spirit of the three wisemen, Amish people exchange gifts.

Datt hands me a large shoebox wrapped in bright green paper. I rip it open. Inside is a pair of used hockey skates. Off come my shoes as I try them on. "If they're too big, wear an extra pair of socks," Datt says.

They feel so good I decide to keep them on awhile. I can't wait to get to the pond.

Jake inspects his new pocketknife. He has fun pulling out all the little gadgets and small tools. Fannie unwraps pretty paper to find a black pocketbook, just like Mamm's.

Rachel waits patiently. But the table is empty except for Mamm's gift. Did Datt and Mamm forget her?

Just then, Datt goes to the sofa and lifts something big and round from under it. "This should make you smile," he says.

"*Danke*," she says, and glows seeing her new snow saucer.

Datt gives Mamm a big roaster pan. She gives him a new wallet. We give Datt a book of our family's genealogy and Mamm a small wooden wall rack with a little mirror and a holder for a kerosene lamp.

Before noon, Datt hitches Roy to the buggy and we drive over to Uncle Steve's place for Christmas dinner. Several buggies are already parked nearby. My cousins must be here! I quickly unhitch Roy and lead him to the barn.

The regular kitchen table is now twice its normal size and it is filled with bowls of many different vegetables. Aunt Lizzie sets the steaming roasted turkey in the middle. *"Kumme esse* (Come eat)," she says. Jake and I find places with the men on one side of the table. Fannie sits with the women on the other side. Rachel and the younger children sit at small tables beyond the kitchen. After a moment of silent prayer, the men start passing one plate after another, while mothers help the children.

After dinner, my cousins and I race to the pond where the boys get up a hockey game. I can really go fast in my skates.

Rachel takes off down the hill on her new snow saucer.

Mamm and Datt stay inside and visit with the grown-ups. Late in the afternoon, we return home to milk the cows.

That evening, Jake hitches his horse to his open buggy. He is driving over to Johnny Kauffman's place where the teenagers are getting together for a "singing."

I've settled in a chair near the wood stove with my new book when there is a knock at the door. English neighbors stop by with a tin of Christmas cookies. Everyone sits around talking, sharing stories, laughing, and eating cookies. Fannie takes out her harmonica and begins to play "Away in the Manger" and soon everyone is singing.

The Second Day of Christmas begins the same as always with chores—milking, collecting eggs, and feeding the animals. Afterwards, I finally get to read my new book.

" *'Siss widder am schneea* (It's snowing again)," Datt says, looking out the window.

Later, I help Datt hitch Roy to the sleigh. The family climbs in, Datt gives the lines a jingle, and across the fields we go. Rachel giggles as the blowing snow tickles her face.

When we arrive at Uncle Amos's place, Grossdawdy and Grossmommy come to the kitchen from their attached house to greet us. Grossmommy gives us each a bag of homemade candy. I eat my favorite chocolate-covered pretzels first, but Rachel likes the chocolate-coated peanut butter balls best.

We can't wait to go outside. Jake and Cousin Ike help me build a fort. We're not quite finished when a snowball knocks off my hat. It's my cousin Omar. Suddenly, it's a free-for-all with snowballs whizzing in every direction.

Fannie, Rachel, and Cousin Emma make a snowman. On its head they place an old straw hat and give him a beard of straw.

That evening I find the place in my new book where I left off. The warm fire in the stove and a full day playing in the cold catch up with me, and I struggle off to bed with heavy eyes.

Unlike English people, we Amish return to school between Christmas and New Year so we can get out of school early in the spring to help with plowing.

So, the next morning, after milking, Rachel and I walk to school. In one hand we each carry our lunch pails. I pull my sled with my other hand, and Rachel drags her snow saucer.

At school the boys and I coast down our long, fast, bumpy trail. Our black hats sail off like Frisbees. Rachel and the girls, on their sleds and snow saucers, slide down a not-so-daring hill.

That evening after our chores, many of the scholars of Sugar Maple School hurry to Uncle Steve's pond. There we build a big bonfire and skate until we can hardly stand.

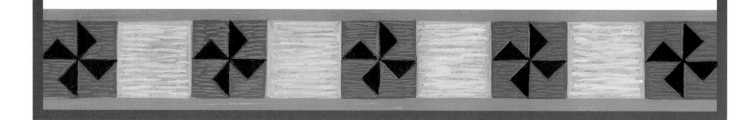

Rachel and I walk home through the snow-covered cornfield. At the crest of the hill, I pause and gaze up at the starry winter sky, knowing this is the same sky that looked down upon baby Jesus. Knowing, too, that this has been the best Christmas, ever.